Kim

Age: 22

Hobby: playing in a rock band with her brothers

Future Goal: FBI agent

Pet at Home: black cat named Chip

Best Quality: fearlessness

THE
SOLDIER

M.G. HIGGINS

SADDLEBACK
EDUCATIONAL PUBLISHING

red rhino
b OO k s™

With more titles on the way …

SADDLEBACK
EDUCATIONAL PUBLISHING
www.sdlback.com

Copyright ©2014 by Saddleback Educational Publishing

ISBN-13: 978-1-62250-901-0
ISBN-10: 1-62250-901-3
eBook: 978-1-63078-033-3

Printed in Guangzhou, China
NOR/0714/CA21401177

18 17 16 15 14   1 2 3 4 5

Leyla

Age: 11

Hobby: collecting wildflowers from the desert with her friends

Future Goal: to go to college in France

Most Disliked Chore: washing dishes

Best Quality: determination

1

IRAQ, 2004

When I was a young girl, my village was in one piece. Now I am twelve. My village is broken. I walk to the water pump with my pail. I rush past the house where Abra lived. I spent much time there. Now only a pile of bricks remains.

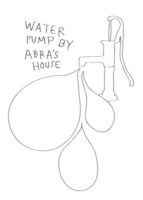

WATER PUMP BY ABRA'S HOUSE

Abra and I played together. She was my best friend. Then a bomb went off. Her father died. So did her brother. Abra and her mother moved away. I don't know where they went. She didn't have time to say good-bye.

I stop in the alley between two buildings. I study the market. My father taught me to do this. Every day my mother reminds me. I need to see who is there. Make sure things are peaceful. As usual, there are three U.S. soldiers. GIs. They carry big guns. They walk calmly. They say *"al salaam a'alaykum"* to the men and women. They give candy to the children. Hakim kicks a soccer ball to Mika. The ball gets away. A GI picks it up. He tosses it to them.

I take a big breath. Leave the alley. Walk to the water pump. Set the pail under the spout. Move the crank up and down. Water gushes out. The pail fills quickly. I lift it with both hands. It is heavy. I walk away as fast as I can. I am supposed to go right home.

"You are very strong," a GI says to me in Arabic.

It is not good Arabic. Just good enough to understand. But that is not what makes me stop. It is the voice. A woman's voice.

All GIs look alike. They wear helmets. They wear bulky brown uniforms. Could one be a woman? I glance up. Pink, smooth skin. A friendly smile. Friendly eyes. Yes, a woman.

I look at the ground. My father would scold me if he saw me with a GI. I get going again. Carry the pail to my house. Water sloshes as I lift it up the porch stairs. I pour the water into a big container. All the while I'm thinking about the woman GI. Does she live with the men? Has she shot that gun? Has she killed anyone? Her life is so different from mine. It is hard to imagine.

That night I ask my father about the woman. His face turns sour. "It is not right. Women should not be soldiers. Another reason they should not be here." He looks me in the eyes. "Stay away from her. Do you understand? Stay away from all Americans."

I nod. I trust him. He is my father. I do what he says.

MY FATHER IS STERN

BUT WISE

Later, there is a meeting in our house. My father has lots of meetings. My two older brothers, Fadi and Sifet, are there. I don't

2

HIDDEN ROOM

My mother sews. There is a shop in our village. It has been there many years. Bombs have not touched it. The women are glad.

It is morning. Before the war, I would go to school. Now the school is broken. They don't have a teacher. So I go to the sewing shop with my mother. I cut cloth. I snip thread. I sew hems by hand. The women talk. They gossip. I get bored.

MY OLD SCHOOL

"I'm going home," I tell my mother.

She tilts her head. As if she has to think about it. But she says, "Okay. Go straight there." She wouldn't let me go if it was dangerous. But it has been two months since our village saw fighting. The GIs fought their way in. Now they say they are keeping the peace. So far, it has been peaceful.

I leave the sewing shop. But I don't go straight home. I stop at a small building. It is between the shop and our house. It is a single room. The roof is damaged. There is a big hole high in the back wall. The family that lived here moved out.

Two weeks ago, I moved in.

The family left no furniture. I found a large wooden box. It is an old crate. I brought my colored pencils. My pad of paper. My eraser. They were birthday gifts from my grandmother. I sit on the floor. I use the box as a table.

I love to draw. When I draw, I am not afraid. I am not even here. I am in another world.

I sketch whatever is in my mind. Perhaps something from a dream. I like animals, so I draw them. Dogs and camels and birds. Today I open my pad to a new page. I start to draw the woman GI's face. I am not very good at faces. But she has stayed on my mind. I think that means I need to get her on paper.

I finish the drawing. Hold up the pad. It is not quite right. Something about her eyes. Her cheeks. She is prettier than what I drew. I would need to see her again to be sure.

With a jolt, I remember the time. Time is out of whack in my drawing world. My mother will be home for lunch. She will be angry if I'm not there. I slide my pad, pencils, and eraser under the box. I run home. She comes home a few minutes later. We make lunch for my father and brothers. My mother and I eat. Then it is time to get water.

LUNCH FOR FATHER & BROTHERS

"Watch, Leyla. Be careful," she reminds me. "Come straight home."

I nod. I head down the porch stairs with my pail. I stand in the alley. I study the marketplace. I look for the woman GI.

3

FACE

It is not a real market anymore. Before the war, there were many stalls. People sold many things. Vegetables. Fruit. Meat. Clothing. Some sellers have come back. Today a man sells melons and potatoes. Another man sells eggs. But it is nothing like before.

Three boys play soccer. Two girls fill a pail at the water pump. They are sisters. They are younger than me. I don't know them well. As usual, there are three GIs. Rifles on their shoulders. They walk in an easy way. But their eyes see everything. One of them is shorter. Smaller. Is it the woman? I think so. The GI turns. I see her face. It is her.

THEY SEE EVERYTHING

I start for the pump. Then stop. The two bigger GIs have changed direction. They walk toward each other. They lean their heads together. Whisper. One punches the other in the arm. They laugh. The smaller GI is nearby. Close enough to hear. She shakes her head. Quickly walks away. Slouches against a wall. Stares at the ground. It reminds me of my brothers. When they tease me. They laugh. I walk away. Then I don't feel so good about myself.

I walk to the pump. The two sisters are just leaving. They carry their heavy pail between them. I pump water until my pail is full. I look for the GI. She still leans against the wall.

IT'S HER! THE WOMAN SOLDIER!

I look around for my father. Brothers. Anyone who will scold me. Tell on me. I see no one.

I carry my pail. Water sloshes. She looks up. Her hand reaches for her gun. I step back. Then she sees it's me. She relaxes. Smiles. "*Al salaam a'alaykum*," she says. Then, in rough Arabic, she says, "I saw you yesterday. You are the strong one."

MY MUSCLES ARE STRONG FROM CARRYING WATER EVERY DAY

I nod. Stare into her face. Her jaw is tighter today. I think she is still thinking about the other GIs. I keep looking. Even though I know it is not polite. Yes. I see what I did wrong. Her mouth is wider. Her cheekbones higher. Her eyes are more almond shaped.

Her smile falters. She shrugs. She must not know how to ask what I am doing. Why I study her like an artist studies their subject. I don't know how to explain. Now I am ashamed for staring.

I say in my language, "Thank you. Good-bye."

I pick up my pail. Carry it home.

Then I join my mother at the sewing shop. I get bored faster than usual. I ask to go home. She says, "Okay."

My quick feet carry me to my hidden room. From under the box, I pull out my drawing supplies. I flip to a new page. I decide to start fresh. The last drawing had too many mistakes. Too much to erase.

I pull out my pencils. Slowly, the GI's face comes to life on the page.

4
MEETINGS

I get home right before my mother again.

She asks, "Leyla, why are your cheeks so red? Are you sick?"

CHEEKS RED

"No. I'm fine."

My cheeks are red because I ran. Also, because I am happy with my drawing. The first portrait I have ever been happy with. I even included the touch of sadness I saw in the GI's eyes. I can never show it to her. Or to anyone. But I think she would like it. I wonder if she likes art. Do people like to draw in America?

We fix dinner. We eat. After dinner my father has another meeting. There are many men in the house. More than usual. My mother and I sit in the kitchen. She mends a shirt. I draw pictures of army trucks. Broken buildings. Broken people. I don't like these drawings. But they are in my mind. So I get them out.

There is a shout in the next room. I jump. So does my mother. Then another shout. It is my father. And my brother Fadi. They are angry. My mother gets up from the table. She takes my hand. "Come," she says. We go out the door. Steps take us up to the roof. We sit on two short stools.

It has been a long time since I was here. We used to watch the stars. I slept here on hot nights. Then it became too dangerous. Soldiers look for snipers on roofs.

"Stay low and quiet," my mother

whispers. She must also be thinking of snipers.

We sit in silence. I see exploding lights to the north. It takes a while for the *boom* to reach us. In the distant west, there is a field of brown tents. The American camp. It is strung with lights. It is bigger than our village. Like a town. I see headlights. A long line of trucks is leaving. I wonder if the woman GI is there. If she is eating. If she is sleeping. Which tent is she in? Does she have family in America? Does she miss them?

"Why would a woman become a soldier?" I ask my mother.

"I don't know," she says.

"Why does Father have so many meetings?"

"That's not for you to know."

"Does it have to do with the war?" I ask.

She doesn't answer.

"Why were they arguing?"

"Keep your voice down."

I sigh. Rub my arms. The breeze is cold. I hear a noise. It is our door opening. Then the sound of feet going down stairs. The door closes.

"They've left," I say.

We climb down from the roof. Father stands in the kitchen. He looks me in the eyes. Frowns. A shiver runs through me. "You are not to get water tomorrow," he says. "You will go to the shop with your mother. You will stay there all day. Do you understand?"

I nod.

He pats my head. Gives me a hard smile. "Don't worry, Leyla. Things will be fine. Things will be better."

I nod again. He is my father. I should trust him.

5

SEWING SHOP

There is the sound of fighting in the night. But it is distant. It is the war in my head that keeps me awake. Images of flying bricks. Crouching in the corner of my room. Praying that my family lives.

I finally go to sleep. I sleep late. My mother shakes me awake. "Come, Leyla. Hurry."

I change my clothes. I go to the kitchen. My father and brothers are not there. My mother hands me an orange for breakfast. She picks up a bag. I think it is our lunch. We leave for the sewing shop. She holds my hand. We walk fast, our heads down.

The shop is full of women and children. It is quiet. The women sit at their machines. They sew. There is little talk. There is no gossip. There is no laughter. My mother hands me a shirt. "Hem, please," she says.

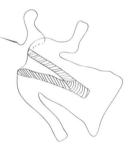

I take the shirt from her. A needle and thread. I sit on the floor. My back against the wall. I stitch. A baby cries. A little boy says, "I want to go home." His mother shushes him.

I am there an hour. Two hours. We are waiting for something. The waiting is awful. The room is hot. There are too many bodies. There is no air. More babies are crying. Children are loud. They are restless. I think I will go crazy. I must get some air. I think I will faint. My mother will not let me go. But I must. I must get out!

I crawl to the door. Open it. I am running. I am taking big breaths of fresh air. I stop at my hidden room.

That is when the fighting starts.

First, gunfire.

Tat-tat-tat-tat-tat.

It is close. In the market.

I hear shouting. Running footsteps. More guns.

There is an explosion. On the road behind me. It is loud. I cover my ears. Crouch in the corner. Shake. This is my father's doing. Him and the other men. They hate the Americans. They want them to go away. My father says we believe in different things. Our beliefs are right. Their beliefs are wrong.

I love my religion. I love my family. But I hate war. I hate how it breaks things.

After the bomb, there is quiet. Then I hear a scream. I have heard this before. Someone is hurt. They are in pain. I press my hands harder against my ears.

More shouting seeps through my fingers. It is in front of my room. Close. Someone runs by the open doorway. I catch sight of a brown uniform. I lower my hands. Whoever it is, they are running the wrong way. That way is a dead end.

I am trembling. But I get to my feet. I peer out. I see a pink face. It is beaded with sweat. It is filled with terror.

6
BATTLE

I hear my brothers' voices. They are coming this way. I lean my head into the alley.

"Hello!" I call to the GI.

She raises her gun. Her eyes are wide. She sees me. Lowers the rifle.

THUMP
THUMP
THUMP

I wave her over. The heavy footsteps come closer. She pauses only a second.

Then she is inside. I close the door behind us.

She is breathing hard. So am I.

She looks around the empty room. So do I.

The wooden box. I point at it. She nods. I lift it up. Pull out my art supplies. She curls herself into a small ball. I set it over her. I sit. Lean against it. Pull my knees up to my chest. Footsteps run past the room. Doors open and slam closed. My door opens. My brother Sifet points a rifle at my head.

"Leyla!" my brother Fadi shouts. He slams his hand down on Sifet's rifle. They both stare at me. They're panting. Faces streaked with dirt. "What are you doing here?"

I don't answer. By now I've wrapped my arms around my knees. I'm rocking back and forth. I'm crying. It has just hit me how scared I am.

"You should be in the sewing shop!"

I nod.

"A GI came this way," Sifet says. "Did you see him?"

I shake my head.

"Stay here. Until we come for you. Do not leave. Do you understand?" They slip away. Close the door.

My heart has never beaten so fast. I think it might explode. Air gushes in and out of my chest. I take the deepest breath I can. Then another. I unwrap my arms from my legs. My hands shake. I lift up the box.

The woman GI sits up. She looks at me. She scoots back until she hits the wall. She presses her face into her hands. I listen to her ragged breathing. Soon she breathes slower. She lowers her trembling hands. She looks at me again.

She says something I don't understand. Then she says, "*Shukran jazilan*." She's thanking me. "You are the strong one," she adds.

I nod. But I think, *No. I am the stupid one. I disobeyed my father. I disobeyed my mother. I am hiding an American GI. What*

will happen if they find out? How will I explain?

The GI points to herself. "Kim," she says. That must be her name.

I pause. "Leyla."

There is more gunfire. Another bomb blast. Dust falls from the ceiling. We cover our heads with our arms. I sit against the wall near Kim. Perhaps we will both die today. Then I will not have to decide what to do next.

7

ALIVE

I am not sure how long the battle lasts. Minutes? Hours? All I know is that the gunfire stops. The explosions stop. And we are still alive.

I am worried about my mother. My father. My brothers. Part of me doesn't want to leave this room. I am afraid of what I will see. More broken buildings. More broken people.

LOOKING THROUGH HOLE

Kim and I have not spoken. I wonder what she's thinking. What she plans to do. There is still daylight outside. If the Americans have won, she might be okay. If my father has won, she will be shot. Ideas run through my head. I should wait for someone to get me. That is what my brother said. But what if my brothers are dead? The thought sickens me. But I must find out what happened.

I get up. I speak simply. Slowly. I hope she understands.

"You hide." I point at the box.

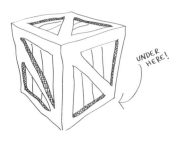

UNDER HERE!

She looks at the box. Looks back at me.

"I go home. Come back. Bring food. Water. News."

Her jaw tightens. Her forehead creases. I can tell she doesn't want to depend on me, a girl. An enemy girl. But she nods. "Thank you."

I lift the box for her. She crawls under it.

I open the door. Peek outside. Dust and dirt fill my nose. The smell of explosives. I run. Stay low. Jump over rubble. Look straight ahead. I do not want to see what is around me. I am too afraid. I get to my house. It is still there. Thank God. I run up inside.

My mother is there. I am so happy to see her. I run into her arms.

"Fadi went to get you," she says.

I pull away. "And Sifet? Father?"

"They are on the roof."

They're still alive! I am weak with relief. Then I imagine them on their bellies. Pointing their rifles. "The Americans are gone?" I ask.

"Yes. For now." She frowns. "You should not have left the shop, Leyla. I was very worried."

"I'm sorry. I couldn't breathe. I had to get away."

Fadi runs in. He smiles when he sees me. His smile quickly fades. "I told you to stay put!"

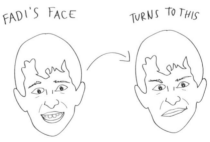

FADI'S FACE   TURNS TO THIS

His response tells me he didn't find Kim. I say nothing.

"I'm going to the roof," he says.

"Here." My mother hands him food. He takes it and is gone.

My mother makes us a simple dinner. I cannot eat. I wonder how many people have died today. I am afraid to ask. I am afraid to think about the future. What will happen to our village? Will the Americans leave us alone? I think of those brown tents. Those trucks. Those planes. Those guns. Those bombs. All of those GIs. One of them is hiding only a few houses away. And it's my fault.

What have I done?

8

ARTISTS

I promised Kim I would return. I promised I would bring food. Water. News.

Now I wonder. This is my family. They are all I have. I should tell my mother about the woman GI.

But I don't want Kim to die. I cannot let that happen.

How will I do this? There are fighters on

the roof. There are fighters on the ground. I wait until dark. My mother is in bed. I dress in my *abaya*. It is black. It will help hide me. I fill a jar with water. I break off a chunk of bread. I take cheese.

JAR
OF
WATER

CHUNK
OF
BREAD

WEDGE
OF
CHEESE

The moon is almost full. I cast a shadow. I stay close to the walls. I walk light on my toes.

I knock quietly on the door. It has been hours since I last saw her. I doubt she is still hiding under the box. I do not want her to shoot me. I open the door a crack. "It is me. Leyla."

I step inside. Close the door. The moon shines through the hole in the ceiling. She stands in the corner. Her rifle in her hands. "You came," she says.

I hold the food and water out for her.

She loops the rifle over her shoulder. First she drinks. Then she says, "Thank you."

Something sits on top of the wooden box. My pad of paper. It is turned to my drawing of her. My cheeks warm.

She eats the bread and cheese. Glances at the pad. "Those pictures are good," she says in her rough words. "You are a good ..." She doesn't finish the sentence. She must not know the word for *artist*.

I say the word for her.

She repeats it. Then she says, "I did this in school. But different." She pretends she's holding something in her hand. She moves her hand up and down, around. I think she means she painted.

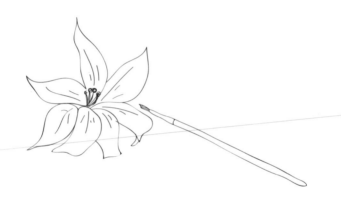

"You really are good," she says. "Better than me. Do you want to be an ... artist?"

I sit on the box. Pick up the pad. I am not sure what she means. To *be* an artist. Does she mean as in work? When I grow up? The way my mother sews? Is that even possible? I would not know where to begin. It makes me think of Kim. How she is a soldier.

"Do you want to be a soldier?" I ask.

"Yes."

"Why?"

She pauses. "For my country. And my father was a soldier."

"He told you to be a GI?"

She sits on the box next to me. "No. My choice. It is what I want. What I always wanted."

I think about this. How strange it seems. "You learned Arabic. To help you be a soldier?"

"Yes." She tilts her head toward the door. "What is going on out there?"

I look away.

"GIs lost the battle?" she asks.

I nod.

Her shoulders sag. She is quiet. She sighs. "I cannot stay." She gets to her feet.

"No!" I tug her sleeve. "Fighters are everywhere."

"I need to get back to my people. I put you in danger."

I stand. "That is my choice."

Our eyes meet. She studies me. Like an artist studies her subject. "You have an idea?" she asks.

SOLDIER KIM'S ALMOND
EYES STUDY ME

"Yes. Do not leave." My quick feet carry me home.

9

ENEMIES

It is very late. From the street, the house is dark. I walk up the steps. Reach for the door. I hear voices. My father's voice. Others. His meetings never interested me. Tonight this one does. I press my ear to the door.

"They will send a drone," I hear Fadi say.

"But they don't know where to attack," Sifet says. "They will not destroy the whole village."

"Sifet is right," my father says. "We stay separated. We fight from every roof. From every corner."

"Do you want our families to die?" It's Fadi again. "This is useless."

"You are a baby." Sifet spits the words out.

"That's enough," my father says.

Another man says, "Amar said trucks are coming."

"We will be ready," my father says. "Let's go."

I step back. They will come this way. I run down the steps. Hide around a corner. The door opens. Some men go up to the roof.

Others come near me. I lower my head. Hold my breath. They pass by.

I wait for my heart to slow. I go back up the stairs. Listen at the door. Silence. I open it a crack. The kitchen is empty. I step into my mother's room. Hope she is asleep. I pull a drawer open. It makes a soft scraping noise. I take what I need. Close it.

"Leyla?" she says.

I stop.

"Is something wrong?"

"I … I can't sleep."

"Neither can I."

She pats the bed. I drop what I'm holding. Lie next to her. She wraps her arm around me. "You're wearing your abaya?"

I think quickly. "Yes. I am afraid. That we might need to leave in a hurry."

She strokes my arm. "I am afraid too. But we have to trust. And we have to sleep. We have to be ready for tomorrow."

I hope she can't feel my heart pounding. She must not. Her breathing slows. As I wait for her to sleep, I think about trust. About my friend Abra. About her father and brother who died. I wonder if her father told her, "Trust me. Everything will be fine."

PHOTOGRAPH ABRA KEEPS OF HER BROTHER

Soon my mother is snoring. I roll off the bed. Pick the bundle up off the floor. Leave through the kitchen. Stand on the top step. Think about my father on the roof. I should not disobey him. I should not defy him.

But I go downstairs. Hug the wall outside. Make my way. Then knock lightly.

"Kim," I say. "It is me. Leyla."

10
AWAY

Kim pulls my mother's abaya over her head. Puts on the *hijab* I brought. It hides everything. Even her rifle. But she is taller than my mother.

HER BOOTS WILL GIVE HER AWAY

"Your boots," I say, pointing at her feet. "People will see. Here." I take off my slippers. Slide them to her.

They are tight. But she squeezes into them. She gives me her boots.

We sit for a long time. Then I say, "GI trucks are coming. You want them to see you're a woman. Both our people. Yours and mine. You should wait till dawn."

"Yes. I agree."

We both glance at the hole in the wall. The sky is not so dark. The night is ending.

Kim turns to me. "I wish I could repay you."

I think. "My village is broken. I don't want it broken more."

She pauses. Nods. "I will talk to someone. I will try."

"There is a person in the village," I tell her. "His name is Fadi. He may help you. I think he wants to talk. Not fight."

"Good to know. Thanks."

I point at the hole in the wall. "That is the best way out."

We move the box. She climbs on top. Turns to me. "Thank you, Leyla." She touches her fingers to my cheek. "You *are* strong. Stronger than anyone I know."

The sun is rising as she crawls outside. She walks slowly. Head down. She could be any village woman. I hear the trucks before I see them. She is at the road now. I hold my breath. A truck slows. Stops. A door swings open. She jumps inside. The truck turns. Goes in the other direction. Dust flies behind it. I trust she will talk to someone. I trust they will listen.

I head for the door. I need to get home. But I stop. On the box is my art pad. It is turned to a new page. A new drawing.

It is a drawing of me.